A Note to Parents and Caregivers:

Read-it! Readers are for children who are just starting on the amazing road to reading. These beautiful books support both the acquisition of reading skills and the love of books.

 The PURPLE LEVEL presents basic topics and objects using high frequency words and simple language patterns.

 The RED LEVEL presents familiar topics using common words and repeating sentence patterns.

 The BLUE LEVEL presents new ideas using a larger vocabulary and varied sentence structure.

 The YELLOW LEVEL presents more challenging ideas, a broad vocabulary, and wide variety in sentence structure.

 The GREEN LEVEL presents more complex ideas, an extended vocabulary range, and expanded language structures.

 The ORANGE LEVEL presents a wide range of ideas and concepts using challenging vocabulary and complex language structures.

When sharing a book with your child, read in short stretches, pausing often to talk about the pictures. Have your child turn the pages and point to the pictures and familiar words. And be sure to reread favorite stories or parts of stories.

There is no right or wrong way to share books with children. Find time to read with your child, and pass on the legacy of literacy.

Adria F. Klein, Ph.D.
Professor Emeritus
California State University
San Bernardino, California

Editor: Jill Kalz
Designer: Nathan Gassman
Page Production: James Mackey
Associate Managing Editor: Christianne Jones
The illustrations in this book were created with watercolor.

Picture Window Books
5115 Excelsior Boulevard
Suite 232
Minneapolis, MN 55416
877-845-8392
www.picturewindowbooks.com

Printed in the United States of America.

Library of Congress Cataloging-in-Publication Data
Williams, Jacklyn.
Pick a pet, Gus! / by Jacklyn Williams ; illustrated by Doug Cushman.
p. cm. — (Read-it! readers. Gus the hedgehog)
Summary: Billy has always had the best show-and-tell presentations, but when Gus
finally gets a pet he is sure it is his turn to shine.
ISBN-13: 978-1-4048-2712-7 (hardcover)
ISBN-10: 1-4048-2712-9 (hardcover)
[1. Pets—Fiction. 2. Snakes—Fiction. 3. Show-and-tell presentations—Fiction. 4.
Hedgehogs—Fiction.] I. Cushman, Doug, ill. II. Title. III. Series.
PZ7.W6656Pic 2006
[E]—dc22   2006003383

Pick a ~~WITHDRAWN~~ Pet, Gus!

by Jacklyn Williams
illustrated by Doug Cushman

Special thanks to our advisers for their expertise:

Adria F. Klein, Ph.D.
Professor Emeritus, California State University
San Bernardino, California

Susan Kesselring, M.A.
Literacy Educator
Rosemount–Apple Valley–Eagan (Minnesota) School District

PICTURE WINDOW BOOKS
Minneapolis, Minnesota

"Guess what I want for my birthday tomorrow, Mom!" Gus said at breakfast.

"A pet," said Mom.

"How did you know?" asked Gus.

"Because that's what you ask for every year, dear," Mom said.

"Can I have one?" asked Gus.

"I'll think about it," Mom said.

At dinner, Gus asked, "Have you finished thinking yet?"

"Not quite," Mom said. "What kind of pet do you want this time?"

"I'll show you tomorrow," Gus said, "when we visit the pet store!"

The next day, Gus and his mom drove to the pet store.

"Welcome to Puggle's Pets," said a short, square man. "My name is Mr. Puggle. May I help you?"

"Today is my birthday," Gus said. "We've come to buy a pet."

"What kind of pet are you looking for?" asked Mr. Puggle.

"I have all kinds of pets," Mr. Puggle continued. "I have snails and hermit crabs. I have birds of all sizes and colors. I also have playful goldfish, clown fish, and angelfish."

Gus' mom shook her head. "Snails and crabs aren't very playful," she said, "and birds are messy, dropping their feathers and seeds. Fish are quiet and clean, but they stare at you impolitely."

Gus pressed his nose against a glass container and smiled. "This is the pet I want," he said. "He looks clean. He's quiet. And I bet he's never impolite. Can I bring him home?"

Gus' mom sighed and said, "OK."

As soon as he got home, Gus started building a house for his new pet.

"You will have to stay in the box until I'm done," he said.

An hour later, Gus was finished.

"See?" he said. "It says 'Gunther' on top. That's your name!"

Gunther made a sound like a leaky balloon. He was happy with his new home.

Gus' friend Bean poked his head over the fence. "What are you doing, Gus?" he asked.

"I'm teaching Gunther some new tricks," said Gus. "So far, he can stay, play dead, and open his mouth when I tap on his back."

GUNTHER

"Can he do anything else?" asked Bean.

"Sure! At night, he sleeps with me and keeps the monsters away. And at dinner, he eats my vegetables so I can have dessert," Gus said.

"Too bad Gunther doesn't know any funny tricks," said Bean. "We could play a joke on Billy."

Gus scratched his head and thought.